*This book
is dedicated
to the child
within all of us.*

Eleventh printing, 2007

Published in the United States of America
Printed by Tien Wah Press in Singapore
Design by Molly Murrah, Murrah & Company, Kirkland, WA

✮ ✮ ✮ ✮ ✮ ✮

Library of Congress Cataloging in Publication Data

Written by Chara M. Curtis, 1950-
        All I see is part of me / words by Chara M. Curtis :
Illustrated by Cynthia Aldrich.
            p.m.
        Summary: A little boy discovers that all of creation is a part of him
and he is a part of creation.
        ISBN 0-935699-07-4 : $15.95
        [1. Self perception—Fiction. 2. Stories in rhyme.] I.
Aldrich, Cynthia, 1947-   III. Title
PZ8.3.C934A1 1989
[E]—dc20

ILLUMINATION
Arts
PUBLISHING CO., INC.

P.O. Box 1865 ✮ Bellevue, WA 98009
(425) 644-7185 ✮ fax (425) 644-9274 ✮ (888) 210-8216 (orders only)

All I See Is Part Of Me

Written by Chara M. Curtis
Illustrated by Cynthia Aldrich

I am part of all I see,

And all I see is part of me.

I am my hands, I am my feet.

I am the puppy across the street.

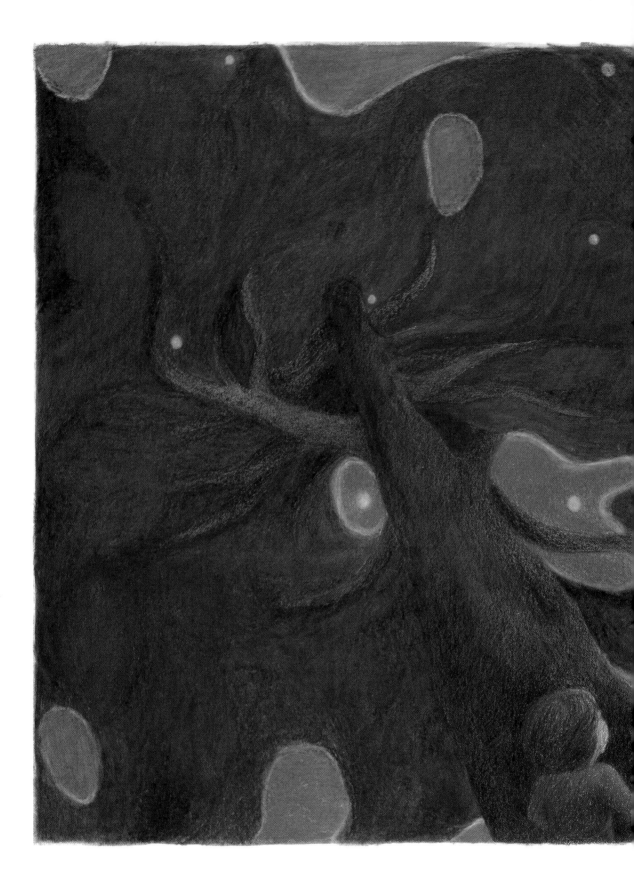

I am the moon,

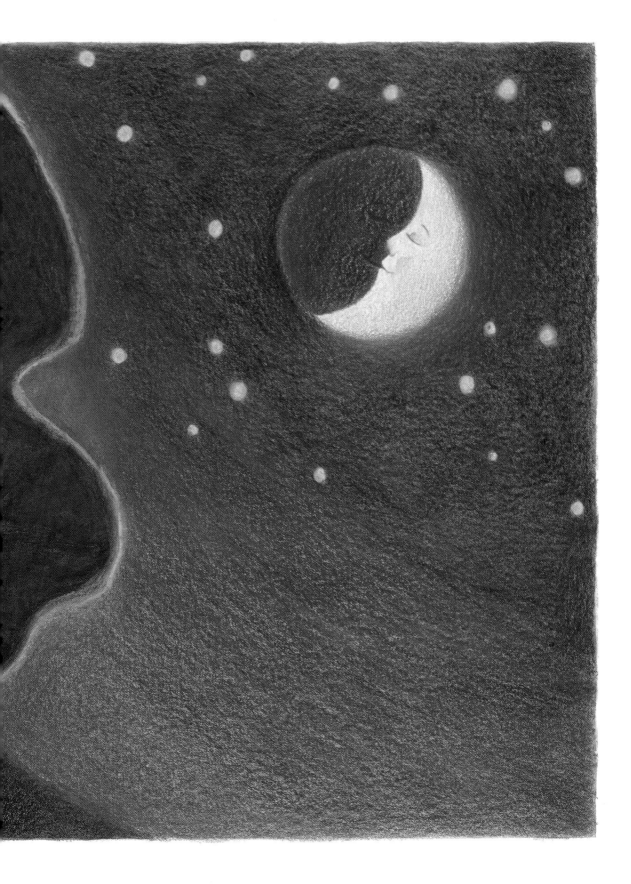

I am the stars.

I'm even found in candy bars!

I used to think that I was small…

A little body, that was all.

But then one day I asked the Sun,
"Who are you?"

He beamed, "We are one."

"But Mr. Sun, how is this true?
How can I be both me and you?"

He smiled, "You might ask your Sister Star.
She, too is part of who you are."

And so I waited 'til the night,
When darkness let me see her light.

"Sister Star, how can it be
That I am you and you are me?"

She glowed, ''You're larger than you know;
You are everyplace there is to go.

You have a body, this is true…
But look at what's inside of you!''

I closed my eyes to see within.
I saw a light! It made me grin.

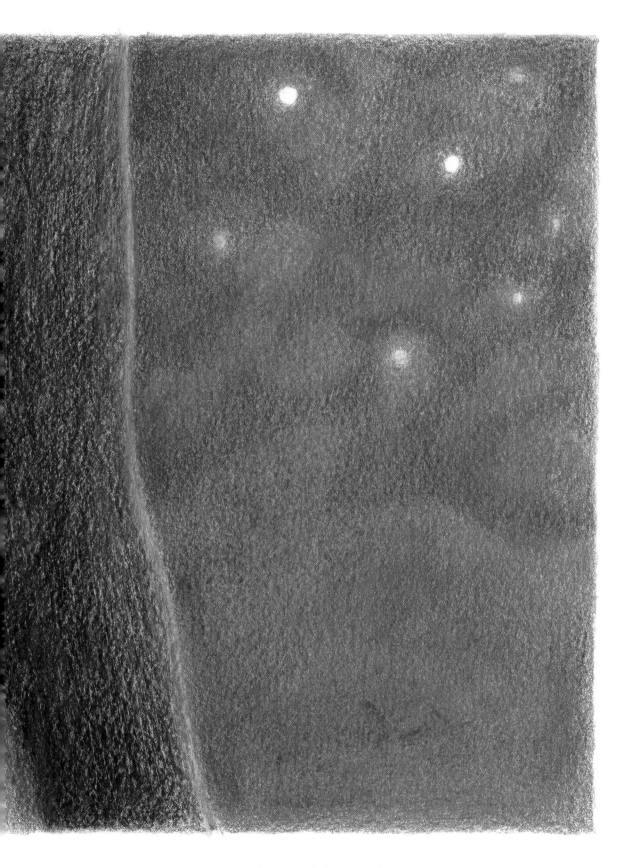

It reminded me of Sister Star.
She said, "That light is who you are.
Your body is just a little part
Of the light that shines within your heart."

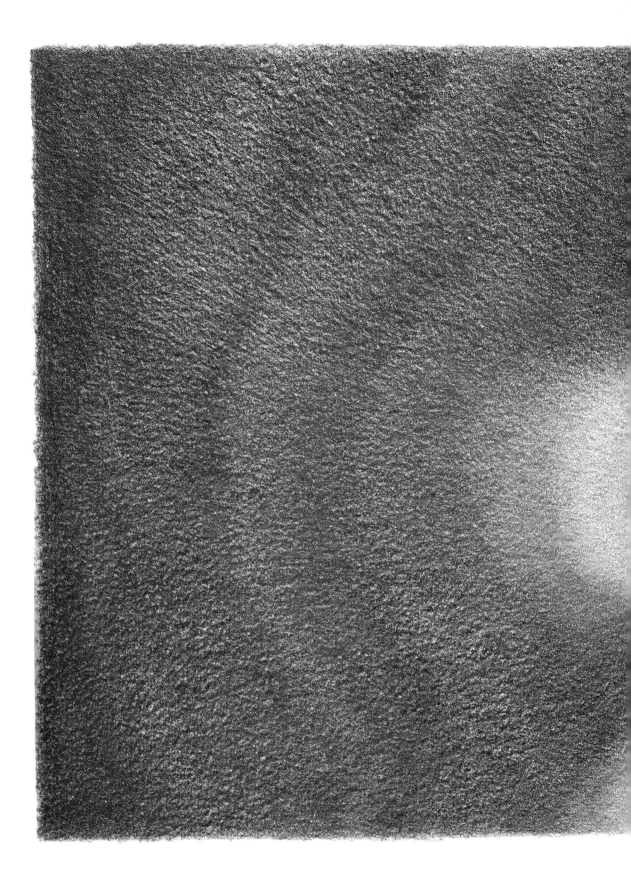

"In all the world, in all of space,
Your light shines bright....It's everyplace!

And when you join it dot-to-dot,
You'll see that *you* is what you've got!"

"All the plants, the animals and trees
Are in your light…and you are these.

Look inside each one you meet,
And see your light....It's so complete!"

''Inside, outside, below, above…
See your light and feel its love.

You're asking *you* when you ask me,
So you know everything, don't you see?"

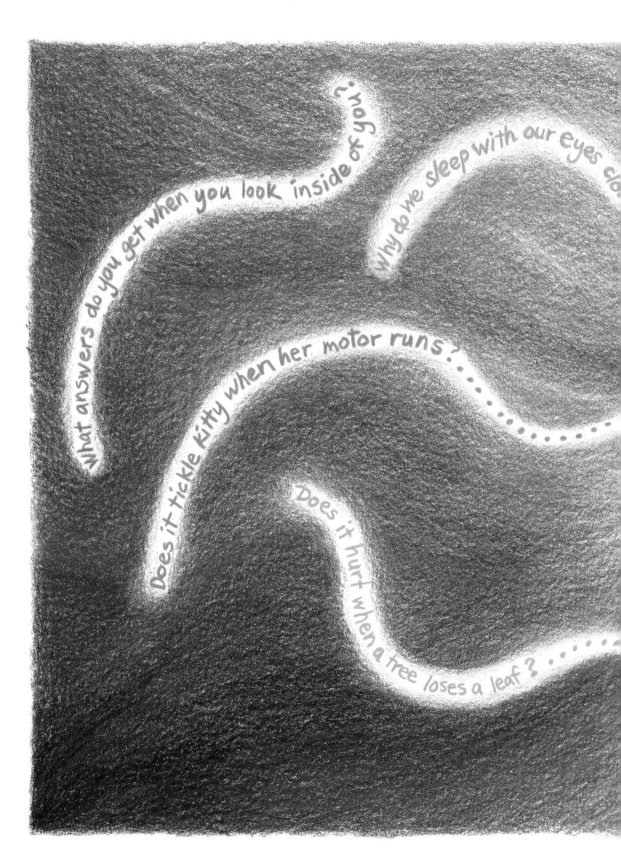

I looked again at all my light
And saw that Sister Star was right.
For every question there could be
The answer is inside of me.

All I ever had to do
Was ask the part of me that knew.

And then I said, "There's something more…
Each question opens up a door.

And every door that I walk through
Leads to a part of me that's new!''

"Thank you so much, Sister Star!
    I love the part of me you are."
    I wondered as I climbed in bed,
    "Does all of me sleep when I rest my head?"

And then a voice…I guess was me…
Replied and spoke most lovingly,
"Even when you sleep, you are
Awake in every shining star."

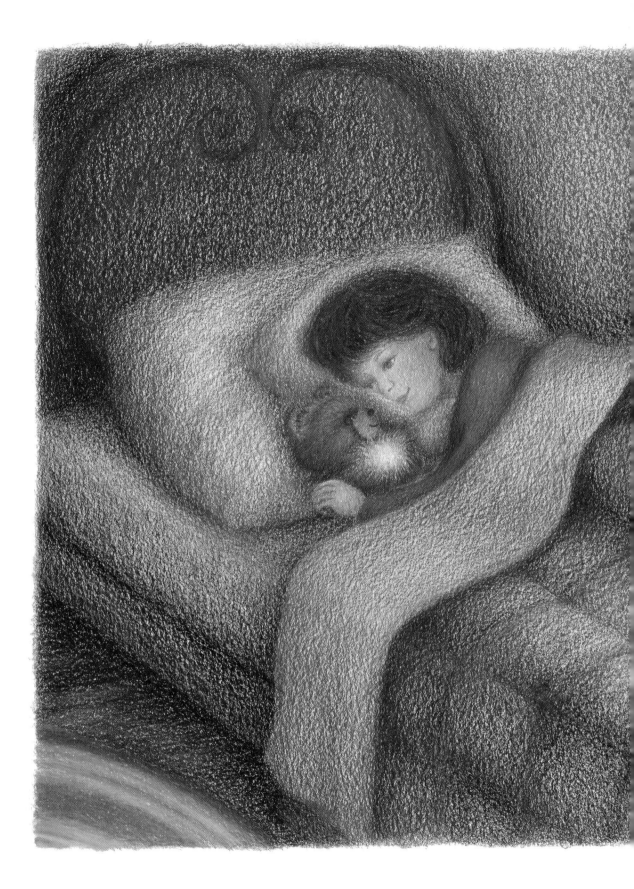

I snuggled with my teddy bear,
And in *his* light, I saw *me* there.

"Open Your Eyes — Your Dreams Are Real..."

"You are me, and I am you.
You love me....I love you, too!"

I closed my eyes and found my light

Dancing with moonbeams in the night.

I said a prayer I know was heard,

'Cause all I am hears every word!

And I can see

In all of me

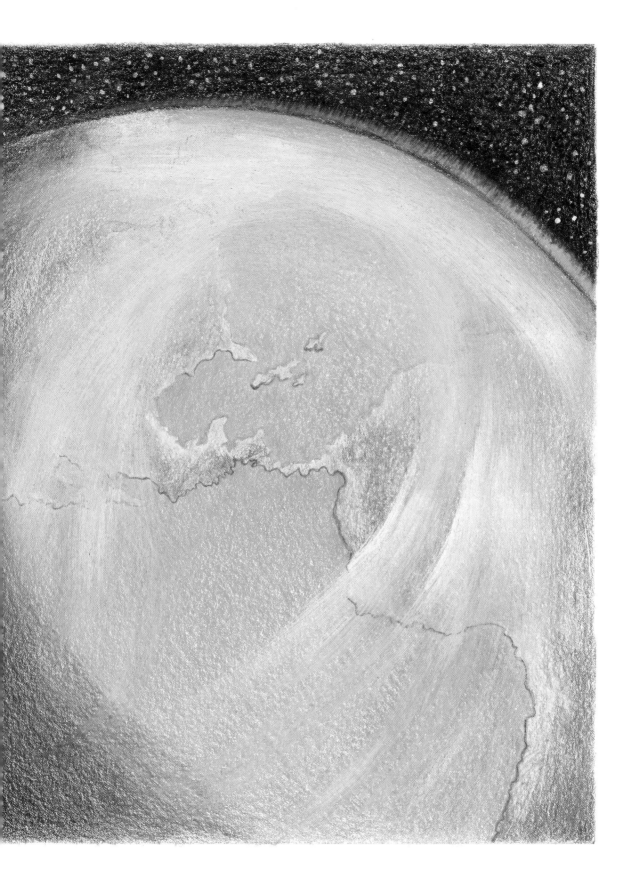

That there can be

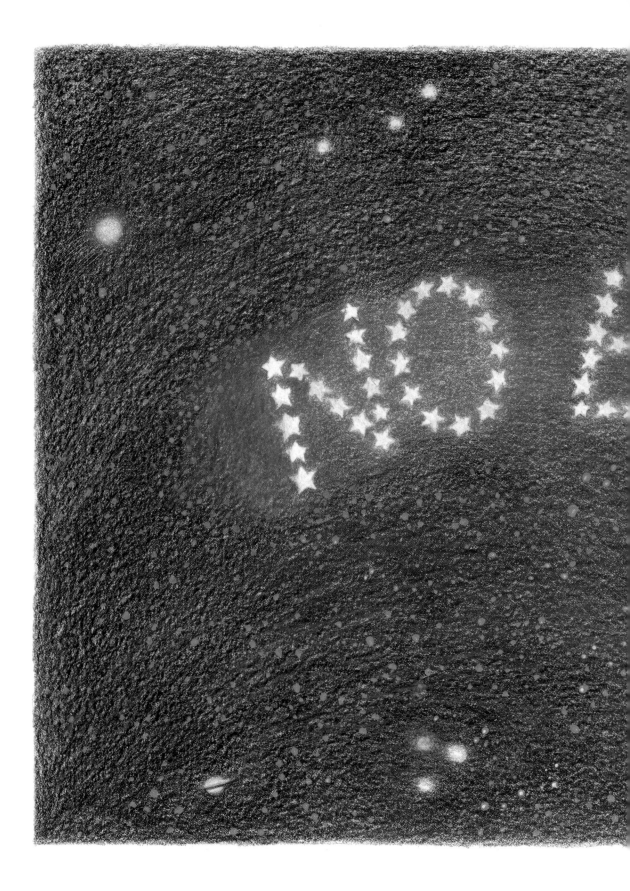

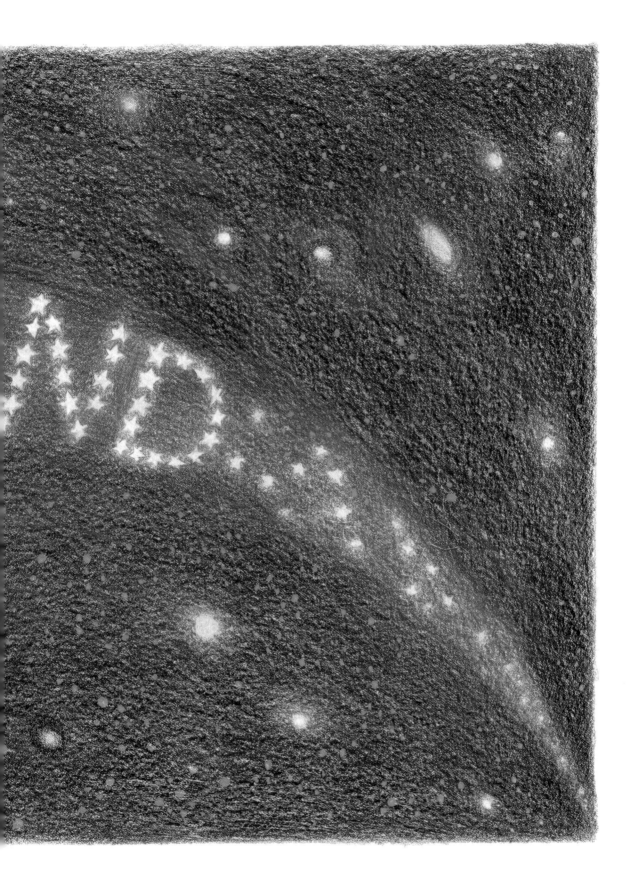

No end…

Chara M. Curtis

Since her Minnesota school days, Chara Curtis has immersed herself in creative writing. After working in advertising and music publishing in Chicago and Nashville, she moved to Northwest Washington State, where writing is her full-time vocation.

Though her expression takes many forms, Chara especially enjoys the process of integrating visual with verbal images. The inspiration for *All I See Is Part of Me* came one sunny day while she was sitting on a river log. "Acknowledging the support of that log, the river, and the surrounding forest evoked a vision of billions of dancing lights of life," she shares. "Everything I saw was of the same essence. I was part of a sea of love and light. Later that evening, I was given the gift of these words. It was a gift meant to be shared."

Chara's published works include two other children's books from Illumination Arts, *How Far to Heaven?* and *Fun Is a Feeling.* In 1997, she received the Washington State Governor's Writers Award for *No One Walks on My Father's Moon.*

Cynthia Aldrich

Born and raised in the Pacific Northwest, Cynthia has always loved to draw and to paint. Since graduating from the University of Washington with a major in painting and graphic arts, she has traveled a number of creative pathways. Her work is displayed in numerous private collections.

Cynthia's present home is in the Four Corners area of Utah. "Living in the Southwest has allowed me to expand into the great outdoors and paint directly from nature," she explains. "This beauty nurtures and inspires me in the creative process."

The rich illustrations in this book were created using multiple layers of colored pencil on textured paper. *All I See Is Part of Me* won an inaugural *Body Mind Spirit Magazine* Award of Excellence in 1996. Cynthia and Chara also collaborated on *Fun Is a Feeling.*

More inspiring picture books from Illumination Arts

Little Yellow Pear Tomatoes
Demian Yumei/Nicole Tamarin, ISBN 0-9740190-2-X, $15.95
Ponder the never-ending circle of life through the eyes of a young girl, who marvels at all the energy and collaboration it takes to grow yellow pear tomatoes.

What If
Regina Williams/Doug Keith, ISBN 0-935699-22-8, $15.95
A little boy uses his fantastic imagination to delay bedtime as long as possible.

The Tree
Dana Lyons/David Danioth, ISBN 0-9701907-1-9, $16.95
An urgent call to preserve our fragile environment, *The Tree* reminds us that hope for a brighter future lies in our own hands.

Your Father Forever
Travis Griffith/Raquel Abreu, ISBN 0-9740190-3-8, $15.95
A devoted father promises to nurture, guide, protect and respect his beloved children.

To Sleep With The Angels
H. Elizabeth Collins-Judy Kuusisto, ISBN 0-935699-16-3, $15.95
"Time to fly with your angel." When a little girl hears these words each night, she knows it's time for wonderful adventures with her beautiful angel.

We Share One World
Jane E. Hoffelt/Marty Husted, ISBN 0-9701907-8-6, $15.95
No matter where we live — whether we work in the fields, the waterways, the mountains or the cities—all people and creatures share one world.

In Every Moon There Is A Face
Charles Mathes/Arlene Graston, ISBN 0-9701907-4-3, $15.95
On this magical voyage of discovery and delight, children of all ages connect with their deepest creative selves.

A Mother's Promise
Lisa Humphrey/David Danioth ISBN 0-9701907-9-4, $15.95
A lifetime of sharing begins with the sacred vow a woman makes to her unborn child.

To view our award-winning collection visit www.illumin.com

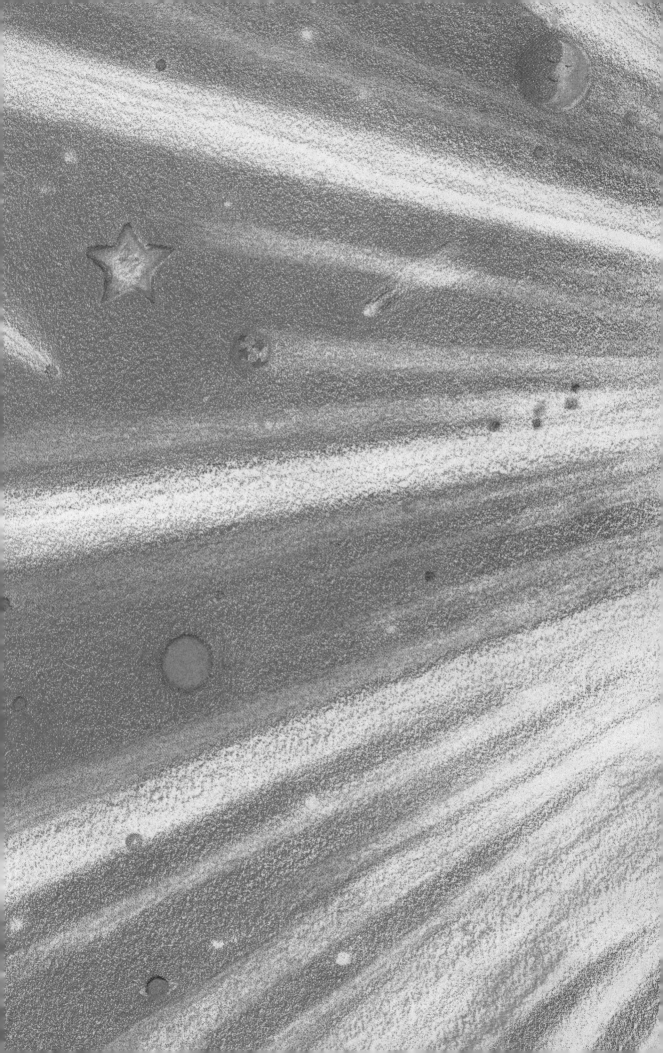